JEWEL KINGDOM

The Sapphire Princess
Meets a Monster

SPARKLE MOUNTAIN

THE GREENWOOD

THE DIAMOND
PALACE

SKATING POND

THE EMERALD
PALACE

THE FOREST
OF FLOWERS

HEART OF
THE WOOD

NANA
WOODBINE'S
COTTAGE

LOOKING
GLASS POND

WILLOW-THAT-WEEPS

THE GREAT OAK

MYSTERIOUS
FOREST

SPINNING
POOL

BLACKWATER BOG

MISTY MARSH

READ ALL THE
JEWEL KINGDOM
BOOKS!

#1: The Ruby Princess Runs Away

#2: The Sapphire Princess Meets a Monster

#3: The Emerald Princess Plays a Trick

#4: The Diamond Princess Saves the Day

JEWEL KINGDOM

The Sapphire Princess
Meets a Monster

by Jahnna N. Malcolm

Illustrations by Sumiti Collina

Scholastic Inc.

This book is a work of fiction. Names, characters, places, and incidents are either the product of the author's imagination or are used fictitiously, and any resemblance to actual persons, living or dead, business establishments, events, or locales is entirely coincidental.

ISBN 978-1-338-56569-0

10 9 8 7 6 5 4 3 2 1   20 21 22 23 24

Printed in the U.S.A.   40
First printing 2020
Book design by Maeve Norton

For Karen Kay Cody
and Princess Gemma

1

THE GOLDEN GIFT

"It's a perfect day for a picnic!" Princess Sabrina said as she sailed across the water in Blue Lake. She was riding in her laurel-leaf boat.

Gurt the gilliwag sat behind her, paddling the boat. The green froglike creature was a close friend of the Sapphire Princess's.

"Princess Sabrina," Gurt said in his deep

voice, "this very golden afternoon matches your golden gift."

That morning a golden basket had very mysteriously arrived at the gates of the Sapphire Palace. A card was pinned to the basket. It read, *To the Sapphire Princess. Signed, A Secret Admirer.*

The golden basket was filled with bread, cheese, and chocolate. Each piece was wrapped in gold cloth and tied with a sapphire-blue ribbon.

Princess Sabrina loved the basket. She had

invited her three cousins to join her for a picnic that afternoon. Demetra, the Diamond Princess, and Emily, the Emerald Princess, had arrived. While they waited for the Ruby Princess, the three cousins sailed across the lake to Bluebonnet Falls.

"Let's have a race!" Sabrina called to the Emerald Princess. Emily was on her knees, paddling a large green lily pad.

"I'm ready when you are," Princess Emily said as she pulled up next to Sabrina. "Just say the word."

Of the four Jewel Princesses, Emily was the most athletic. She ruled the Greenwood and spent her days climbing trees and riding through her lush green forest.

The Diamond Princess steered her boat

made of white gardenias between her two cousins. Demetra ruled the White Winterland, and everything she wore was glittering white.

"I think we should wait for Roxanne," Demetra advised. "Wasn't she going to join us?"

"Roxanne is *always* late," Emily said with a frown. "If we wait for her, it will be sundown before we get to eat."

Sabrina focused her dark brown eyes on the shore. There was no sign of the Ruby Princess.

"I agree with Emily," Sabrina announced. "Let's have a race ourselves."

"No, no, no!" squeaked a yellow-and-pink butterfly as she landed on Sabrina's finger. It was Zazz, Princess Sabrina's palace adviser and best friend.

"Princess, if you race in this boat, you'll lose," Zazz sputtered. "Or sink. Just look at what we're carrying. Gurt. That heavy gold basket. The napkins and tablecloths, and all of the royal china."

Sabrina put her face nose-to-nose with the tiny butterfly. "Then I'll just have to get another boat. Any idea where I might find one?"

Blue Lake was dotted with boats. "I'll call the nymphs," Zazz said as she fluttered off the princess's finger. "They'll bring a leaf boat right over."

"Don't do that," Emily called. "Sabrina, hop on my lily pad. We'll race Demetra together."

Sabrina stood up to leap onto Emily's boat, but something tugged at her arm.

Sabrina spun around. No one was there.

Just Gurt the gilliwag calmly paddling away. She looked at the mysterious golden basket. It glittered in the afternoon sun.

"Come on, Sabrina!" Emily cried. "Jump!"

Before Sabrina could make a move, the basket danced across the bottom of the boat and leaped into her hands.

Emily gasped. "Did you see that?" she asked Demetra.

"I don't like this," Demetra said, shaking her shiny black hair. "Sabrina, you should leave that basket alone. You don't know where it came from."

"Don't be such a worrywart!" Sabrina stared at the golden basket. "This is a present. A very magical present from a secret admirer. Full of wonderful food."

"And I'm starving," Zazz called from her perch on the boat's bow.

"Me too." Sabrina leaned forward and whispered to the butterfly, "Zazz, let's not wait until we get to Bluebonnet Falls. Why don't you and I take a piece of chocolate from the picnic basket right now?"

Zazz rubbed her little legs together. "I like chocolate. Yes, yes!"

Sabrina opened the basket. But just as her fingers touched the food, something jolted the boat.

"Whoa!" Zazz fell backward onto the floor of the boat and bent one antenna. "What was that?"

"I'm not sure!" Sabrina replied.

Thunk! Something hit the boat again.

"I'm afraid something is trying to sink us," Gurt declared, pulling his paddle into the boat.

"The water sprites must be playing a joke." Sabrina peered into the water. She was looking for the ghostly outline of the little sprites.

"If the sprites don't want you to see them, Princess, you won't," Zazz said as she tried to straighten her antenna.

"I'll try calling them." Sabrina cupped her hands around her mouth. "Hello? Anybody there?"

Nothing.

The Sapphire Princess leaned over the

side of the boat. She was so close, her nose nearly touched the lake.

All at once two huge yellow eyes appeared just below the surface.

Sabrina screamed and fell backward.

2

THE BLUE LAKE MONSTER

"Sabrina!" Demetra fanned Sabrina's face with a broad green leaf.

Zazz fluttered nervously over their heads.

"Is the princess all right?" the butterfly asked.

Gurt pointed toward the Sapphire Palace. "Should I swim for help?"

"Please don't. I'm fine!" the Sapphire

Princess said, pulling herself into a sitting position. "I saw a face, and it surprised me!"

Emily squinted one eye closed and peered at her cousin. "What kind of face?"

"A face as big as this boat," Sabrina replied. "It was under the water."

"I'll go see what it was!" Gurt cried. The gilliwag dove over the side and instantly disappeared from sight.

Demetra poured Sabrina a cup of honey nectar. "What did the face look like?"

Sabrina took the cup and slowly sat up. "Well, it was huge and gray. And very lumpy."

"Did it have a mouth?" Emily asked.

Sabrina nodded. "Yes. And its teeth looked razor-sharp."

"What about its body?" Zazz asked, perching on Sabrina's shoulder. "Did you see it?"

Sabrina sipped the nectar. "I didn't see its body, but if its head was as big as this boat, then the body would have to be as big as ten boats."

Zazz frowned. "There's nothing that big

that lives in the lake except..." Her eyes widened. "The Blue Lake Monster!"

They heard a splash behind them and everyone jumped. The gilliwag draped his long green arms over the side of the boat.

"I saw a shadow," Gurt gasped. "I tried to follow, but it disappeared into the Deep Dark."

The Deep Dark was an inky stretch of water where none of the lake folk ever swam. It was very deep and very, very cold.

Now Zazz's eyes were as huge as lily pads. "Then it *was* the Blue Lake Monster!"

Sabrina tapped Zazz on the top of the head with her fingertip. "What's all this talk about a Blue Lake Monster? I've never heard of it."

Zazz shivered. "It's terrible. Just terrible."

"The monster has always been down there," Gurt explained. "Some say it is an evil creature left over from when Lord Bleak ruled the land."

"Lord Bleak!" Demetra gasped. "How awful!"

Lord Bleak and his Dreadlings had been banished from the Jewel Kingdom years before. That was when Queen Gemma and

King Regal had come to the throne. They had divided up the Jewel Kingdom, giving each of their nieces her own jewel and her own land.

"If it has anything to do with Lord Bleak, it must be mean and horrible," Emily said, clutching her cousins' hands.

Gurt shrugged. "I don't know. I've never heard of the monster harming anyone."

"Then maybe it's a friendly monster," Sabrina said.

Zazz put her face close to Sabrina's. "But you said that it was gray and had fierce teeth. That sounds dangerous."

"I think you should warn your people," Demetra advised.

Sabrina didn't like to jump to conclusions.

She preferred to think things over before taking any action. "I just saw a face," she said. "It could have been a sprite playing a trick, trying to scare us."

Zazz reluctantly agreed. "They have been known to do that."

Sabrina smiled at her cousins and friends. "We're almost to Bluebonnet Falls. We were going on a picnic. So why don't we eat our lunch and talk about it?"

She picked up the picnic basket and set it in her lap.

Suddenly, a huge gray head burst out of the water.

"The Blue Lake Monster!" Zazz squealed.

The monster opened its jaws and let loose a terrible roar.

Sabrina dropped the picnic basket and reached for the purse she wore at her waist. Inside was magic dust that the great wizard Gallivant had given her. She tossed the dust over herself and her guests.

"*From water to air,*" she chanted.

Sabrina, Emily, Demetra, and Gurt all rose into the sky. Zazz fluttered beside them.

Sabrina extended one arm to the sky. "*Higher and higher, let us go.*"

The group flew far above the monster's head. From her place in the sky, Sabrina could see the dark shadow of the monster beneath the water. The creature was bigger than she had even imagined. Its body seemed to stretch halfway across the lake.

"What should we do, Princess Sabrina?" Zazz cried. "Where should we go?"

The Sapphire Princess faced her palace, which sat like a bridge over Blue Lake. "Demetra and Emily, fly back to my palace with Gurt. Zazz, come with me."

"But where will you go?" Demetra asked.

Sabrina pointed to the far shore of Blue Lake. "To the storkz. They'll know what to do!"

3

CALL THE STORKZ!

The storkz lived in the Misty Marsh. It was always damp and always covered in a pale green cloud.

"Sage is the leader of the storkz," Sabrina said as they glided into the marsh. "We need to talk to him."

Zazz clung to the sleeve of Sabrina's gown. "I hope we find him soon," the butterfly mumbled. "It's cold and scary here. I can't see two feet in front of me."

"Don't you worry, friend," Sabrina cooed. "There's nothing to fear."

Suddenly, a creature with long yellow legs and a thin body covered in blue feathers

magically appeared out of the mist. Its big round eyes peered at them from behind tiny gold-rimmed glasses.

"*Sage!*" Sabrina gasped.

"Have you been there all along?" Zazz squeaked, hopping to Sabrina's shoulder. "I didn't see you."

"We are all here." Sage gestured with one wing to the clumps of reeds around him.

Sabrina could see dozens of storkz. All standing tall and still.

"We hear through the waters that you are worried about our lake creature," Sage said, staring at her solemnly.

"That's no creature," Zazz cut in. "It's a terrible monster."

"Zazz!" Sabrina tapped the butterfly lightly on her head. "Careful what you say. We're not sure it's terrible."

"The princess is right," Sage advised. "Let's not be too hasty. That creature has lived in Blue Lake a very long time."

"Is it older than the storkz?" Zazz asked, wide-eyed.

Sage nodded. "Much older. It's been here since the beginning."

"That's why it's so big," Zazz whispered in Sabrina's ear. "With all of that time, what else was there to do but grow!"

"This creature has not shown itself to humans in eons." Sage peered over the top of his glasses. "There must be a reason for this."

"Of course there's a reason," Zazz sput-tered. "That awful monster has been sent by Lord Bleak to hurt our princess."

Sabrina wanted to say that wasn't true. But she had to admit, the creature *did* frighten her.

"It attacked my boat," Sabrina told Sage.

"And then it leaped out of the water and roared at me."

"Hmm... This is not good," Sage murmured. "I must talk to the other storkz."

In an instant, all of the pale blue birds vanished from sight.

"Do you think the storkz are still here?" Zazz whispered.

"Yes," Sabrina whispered back. "I can't see them, but I feel them all around us."

"Go back to your palace, Princess," Sage said when he returned. "We will try to speak to the lake creature."

Sabrina bowed to the leader of the storkz. "Thank you. I will do as you say."

"What do you mean, you'll do as he says?" Zazz demanded as they flew back to the

Sapphire Palace. "Sage just wants us to sit and wait!"

"We must be sure about this creature before we scare our people," Sabrina explained. "Promise me, Zazz, that you'll keep this secret."

"Too late," the butterfly said as the palace came into view. "It looks like the secret is out."

Sabrina looked down. The shallow water around the palace was crowded with blue-skinned nymphs and gawky gilliwags. They waved huge willow wands in the air. Big-footed striders skated under the drawbridge, clutching oars in their hands. Even the water sprites, pale and ghostlike, had joined the mob.

"We must all hunt for this monster!" Gurt shouted from the center of the crowd.

"Find the monster!" the crowd shouted back.

"And tell it to get out of our kingdom," Gurt added. "And stay out!"

4

MONSTER HUNT

Princess Sabrina and her cousins huddled together by her bedroom window. Below they could see the crowd guarding the palace.

"It's very sweet that my people want to protect me," Sabrina remarked. "But I'm worried."

"I'm worried, too," Princess Demetra said. "That monster could destroy all of the willow wands with one swift bite."

Sabrina leaned her head against the frame of her open window. She thought about what Sage had told her.

"Why would this monster, who has lived peacefully for so many years, suddenly appear?" she asked the princesses.

"Maybe it wants to tell you something," Emily suggested.

Sabrina nodded. "That's what I've been thinking. But what?"

"I think it wants you to go home. Back to the Jewel Palace," Demetra said. "And that's what I would do if I were you."

Sabrina squeezed her cousin's hand. "I can't leave, Demetra. When I was crowned Sapphire Princess, I promised to protect Blue Lake and all of the creatures who live here."

"Even *that* creature?" Emily pointed at the lake. Just below the surface, as big as a ship, was the Blue Lake Monster!

Demetra backed away from the window.

"Sabrina, I'm scared! Why has it come to the palace?"

Sabrina watched the shadow glide swiftly toward the drawbridge. "It's after my people," she gasped. "I've got to stop it!"

"But how?" Emily cried. "You're just one girl. And that thing is monstrous."

"I have to do something." Sabrina climbed onto the window ledge and peered out. "The gilliwags and the nymphs don't even see it!"

Emily caught hold of Sabrina's ankle. "Careful, you might fall."

Sabrina's big brown eyes widened. "That's it," she said. "I'll jump out of my window and distract it."

"But it will gobble you whole," Demetra warned.

"I won't land in the water." Sabrina patted the little purse at her waist. "I'll use my magic dust and fly across the lake."

"Then the monster will follow you," Emily said.

Sabrina smiled. "That's the idea."

"Do you have enough magic dust to make it across the lake?" Demetra asked.

"If I run out," Sabrina replied, "then I guess I'll have to swim."

Demetra covered her face and groaned. "Oh no."

"I'll lead it near the Willow-That-Weeps," Sabrina said, thinking out loud. "Then maybe it will get caught in the Spinning Pool and disappear forever."

Suddenly, the shadow beneath the water

froze. It slowly turned. Two big yellow eyes
rose to the surface of the lake.

It was looking straight up at Sabrina!

"Sabrina, I don't like your plan," Demetra
said in a shaky voice. "Please climb down
from that window."

Sabrina's gaze was locked with the mon-
ster's. "I can't," she whispered. "It's watching me."

Very slowly, Sabrina opened the purse at her waist. She carefully scooped up a handful of magic dust. All the while, she whispered instructions to the other princesses.

"When I leave, you two go to the courtyard and guard my people," Sabrina murmured, barely moving her lips. "Tell them to stay on land. That's one place we know the monster won't go."

The monster raised its head out of the water. Its big, spiky teeth sparkled in the sunlight.

It's going to get me! Sabrina thought, nearly falling back into the room.

"Oh no," Emily cried.

"I'm okay." Sabrina squeezed her eyes closed and willed herself to be brave. She clutched the side of the windowsill with one hand and faced the monster.

"Sabrina, don't do this," Demetra pleaded. "You have to save yourself!"

"I will," Sabrina replied as she flung the magic dust in the air. "But first I have to save my people."

5

SPARKLE OF LIGHT

Sabrina looked down and smiled. Her plan was working. The monster was following her!

She flew closer to the water to make sure the monster could see her. The big dark shadow mirrored her every move. If she turned, it turned. If she flew faster, it swam faster.

Across the lake Sabrina could see a patch of churning water by the Willow-That-Weeps.

The Spinning Pool! She was about to head for it when something caught her eye.

A sparkle! A very golden sparkle.

Princess Sabrina shielded her eyes with her hand. The golden light was blinding. Where was it coming from?

Flash!

There it was again. Sabrina squinted toward the shore.

"My boat!" she cried. It was caught in the reeds by Bluebonnet Falls. "That golden light is coming from my boat!"

Inside the boat was the golden basket. It was glowing.

Suddenly, Sabrina was being pulled out of the sky!

"What's happening to me?" she cried as the light pulled her closer and closer to shore. "Stop!"

When she was just over the boat, the golden basket leaped into her hands. "My goodness!" she cried in surprise.

Sabrina gently landed on the grassy shore. For a moment, she forgot all about the Blue

Lake Monster. And thought only of the golden basket.

Sabrina knelt and placed the basket in front of her. Carefully, she looked at the gifts.

"Oh!"

There, tied with a sapphire-blue ribbon, was the most beautiful pear the princess had ever seen. Its skin shimmered like polished gold.

She couldn't take her eyes off it.

Sabrina's mouth began to water. Her fingers twitched.

"I have to eat it," she murmured, picking up the pear.

Sabrina was just about to take a juicy bite when she heard a huge splash in the lake.

"Nooooooo!" the monster roared, shooting out of the water. It towered above Sabrina's head. Then it opened its jaws and bent forward.

The princess froze with the pear in midair.

This is it, she thought, staring into the beast's mouth. *It's going to gobble me up.*

She squeezed her eyes shut and waited.

But she only felt a slight tug. At her fingers.

Sabrina opened her eyes and stared at her empty hand.

"My pear!" she gasped.

The Blue Lake Monster had eaten it. The beast had swallowed the golden fruit in one gulp. And now something odd was happening to the monster.

Its gray skin turned green. Then it changed to a sickly yellow.

The monster began to sway, its eyes rolling back in its head. Slowly, slowly, it fell forward.

"Ooomph!"

First the body hit the ground. Then the long neck stretched across the grass.

Finally, the monster's head came to rest, with its nose in Princess Sabrina's lap.

6

THE POISONED PEAR

Sabrina stared at the Blue Lake Monster's head. It was as big as a boat. It lay with its eyes closed, breathing in shaky gusts of air through its nose.

Sabrina carefully reached up and touched the monster's nose. The yellow skin was soft, like the petals of a flower.

The monster sighed at her touch.

"Poor monster," Sabrina whispered. "You're sick."

The ragged breathing grew calmer.

Sabrina's heart went out to this creature. It looked so sad and helpless.

"There's the princess!" a voice cried from behind her. "The monster has her in its clutches."

Sabrina turned to see her cousins rounding the bend by Bluebonnet Falls. They were leading many creatures from Blue Lake.

"Don't worry, Sabrina, we'll save you!" Emily shouted as she hiked up her skirt and raced to help the Sapphire Princess.

Zazz the butterfly clung to the top of Emily's wild red hair and ordered, "Faster! Run faster!"

Gurt and several other gilliwags hopped behind Emily and Zazz, waving wooden oars in the air.

"Save the princess!" Gurt bellowed.

"Stay back!" Sabrina cried, wrapping her arms around the monster's head. She pressed her cheek against its skin. She could hardly hear it breathe. "This creature is sick. Please, don't hurt it."

Princess Emily and the crowd stumbled to a stop. They were confused.

"But ... but I don't understand," Emily stammered. "I thought that monster was trying to hurt you."

Sabrina looked at her cousin with sad eyes. "That's what I thought, too. But I think it was only trying to help me."

Zazz fluttered above the golden basket that had fallen over on its side. The pears had tumbled onto the ground. Dead flies and ants lay around the golden fruit.

"Look, everyone!" Zazz cried. "This food ... it was poisoned."

Demetra narrowed her eyes at the golden

basket. "I knew something was wrong. That gift wasn't from a secret admirer."

"It was from a secret enemy," Emily finished.

"And it was *sooo* beautiful," Zazz finished.

Sabrina stroked the monster's lumpy head. "You knew that pear was poisoned, didn't you? You ate it to save me."

Sabrina thought back to the first time the monster had bumped her boat. It was when she touched the golden basket. Then the monster reared out of the water when Sabrina and Zazz were about to sneak a bite of chocolate.

"We were all wrong," Sabrina announced. "This creature never tried to hurt me. Everything it did was to help me."

The monster moaned and rolled its head to one side.

Sabrina knew it was in great pain. Tears welled up in her eyes.

"You poor thing," she said. "I wish there was something I could do to help you."

"Perhaps there is," a voice whispered across the wind.

Sabrina lifted her head and looked toward the lake. There, half-hidden in the reeds, was Sage.

"At the base of Bluebonnet Falls grows a tiny purple flower," the wisest of the storkz said. "It has the power to heal." The monster groaned again and Sage added, "But you must be quick. There isn't much time."

Sabrina could have asked Gurt, or even Zazz, to go to the falls. But this was one thing she had to do herself.

The monster had saved her life. Now she would return the favor.

7

THE SPIRIT OF BLUE LAKE

The purple flower grew only in one spot, directly behind the waterfall. To pick it, Sabrina had to duck around the rushing water.

Now the princess knelt before the dying monster. Her shoes were soaked and stained with mud. The sleeves of her dress dripped with water. But she didn't care. Sabrina had the magic flower.

It took all her strength to pry open the monster's thick jaws. Finally, she was able to place the flower on its tongue.

"Swallow this," she urged. "It will make you feel better."

Demetra and Emily stood with Zazz and the other lake dwellers at a safe distance. Even though the monster seemed sick, they still didn't trust it.

Sabrina stroked the monster's brow. "Please, try to swallow. I want you to live. You *have* to live."

After a few seconds, the creature swallowed.

"Good. You did it!" Sabrina cheered. "Now relax and let the flower work its magic."

Sabrina and her friends watched and

waited. The cure seemed to take forever. But ever so slowly, the sickly yellow skin turned back into a nice dark gray.

Sabrina kept petting the monster's head. Its breathing was becoming less harsh.

"That's a good monster," she cooed. "You're getting better. I can see it."

A low growl rattled in the monster's throat. And all of the lake dwellers leaped back in alarm.

"Sabrina, be careful!" Demetra warned.

Sabrina ignored her cousin and kept stroking the monster's nose and brow.

With each breath, it seemed to grow stronger. Soon its body began to twitch. Then its eyelids fluttered.

"It's waking up," Sabrina announced.

Demetra, Emily, and the others took another giant step backward.

Sabrina held her breath.

At last the monster opened its eyes. It looked at Sabrina and big tears welled up in its yellow eyes.

"Please, don't judge me by the way I look,

Princess," the creature said in a high, lilting voice.

Sabrina blinked in surprise. The Lake Monster was a girl!

"I'm afraid I might frighten you," the monster continued.

"But I'm not frightened!" Sabrina cried. "I think you're beautiful."

The monster sighed. A deep sigh, full of sorrow. "There was a time when you might have said I was beautiful and everyone would have agreed with you." Her huge eyes narrowed. "That was before Lord Bleak and the Dreadlings ruled this land."

"You mean you haven't always looked like this?" Sabrina asked.

"Oh no," the monster replied in her lovely

voice. "I was once a mermaid with sea-green eyes and skin the color of pearls. I was called Oona."

"Oona!" Zazz blurted. "I've heard stories of Oona."

Gurt nodded. "Oona is the Spirit of Blue Lake. They say she has been here since the beginning of time."

Oona nodded. "That's true."

"But why have we never seen or heard from you?" Sabrina asked.

Oona hung her head. "After Lord Bleak cast his spell on me, my friends didn't recognize me. I scared them and they ran away."

"But we wouldn't run..." Sabrina didn't finish her sentence. She realized that she *had* run from Oona. And so had her people.

"We made a mistake," Sabrina declared, looking at the crowd.

Zazz hung her head. "We were wrong."

Sabrina knelt in front of the huge creature. Demetra, Emily, and all the creatures of Blue Lake knelt, too.

"Dear Oona, will you accept our sincerest apology?" Sabrina asked.

The corners of Oona's gray lips curled into a smile. "Of course. And let me say that after years of hiding in the Deep Dark, at last I can say I am happy."

Everyone cheered. Sabrina stood up and clapped her hands in delight. "Oh, I wish we could celebrate this moment with a feast!"

Gurt stepped forward. "Princess, we still have the china and the tablecloths."

"And all the guests are here," Zazz added.

"That's true. But we have no food to offer anyone." Sabrina pointed to the picnic basket and the poisoned food beside it. "Not one crumb."

Suddenly, a shadow darkened the sky. It swooped over their heads with a rush of wind.

"Look out!" The lake dwellers clutched their heads and huddled in fear.

Sabrina looked up, frightened. But her fear soon turned to joy. She skipped over to her cousins and pointed skyward.

Emily laughed out loud. "Look who's here!"

Demetra opened one eye and peeked at the sky. "Well," she huffed. "It's about time!"

8

FOUR CROWN JEWELS

A great fire-breathing dragon circled above the crowd. Riding on its back, laughing and waving, was Roxanne, the Ruby Princess.

Sabrina raced to greet her cousin as soon as the dragon touched down. "You're here at last!"

Roxanne wore a ruby-red dress complete with a red satin cape. She tossed the cape over her shoulder and hugged Sabrina. "It's so good to see you! Did I miss anything?"

"Miss anything?" Demetra repeated as she and Emily ran to join the princesses. "We've had an entire adventure while we waited for you."

Roxanne's eyes sparkled. "Oh, we love a good adventure." She turned to the green-and-red dragon. "Don't we, Hapgood?"

Hapgood was Roxanne's friend and palace adviser. He lived with the Ruby Princess in the Red Mountains.

The dragon nodded very formally to the princess. "Life with you is one great adventure. I do enjoy it. It keeps me young."

Roxanne patted the dragon's neck. "That's the spirit, Happy."

Emily draped her arm around Sabrina's shoulder. "Look at us. We're all together."

"Yes." Sabrina smiled fondly at her three cousins. "Here we are, the four jewels of our kingdom."

Demetra nodded. "Now we all have a very good reason to celebrate. It's too bad about our picnic, though."

"What happened?" Roxanne asked.

The other three looked at one another. Sabrina spoke first. "It's a very long story. Let me just say that our basket of food was poisoned."

"Who would have done such a thing?" Roxanne asked.

Demetra lowered her voice. "Lord Bleak and his Dreadlings."

"Oh!" Roxanne gasped, putting one gloved hand to her mouth. "Flying here we passed over the Mysterious Forest. Hapgood was certain he saw several Dreadlings running into the woods."

"They wore black capes and seemed upset about something," Hapgood added.

"They were upset because their awful

trick didn't work," Demetra cut in. "They tried to poison Sabrina!"

"Luckily, Oona was there to save me," Sabrina declared.

"Oona?" Roxanne cocked her head. "Who's Oona?"

Sabrina pointed to the spot where the lake creature had been resting. It was empty.

"She was just over there by the shore, but she's gone," Sabrina said. "I hope she didn't run away."

"What does she look like?" Roxanne asked, glancing around.

Before, Sabrina would have described Oona as gray and lumpy with fierce, pointed teeth. But now when she thought of Oona, she could only remember her eyes.

"She has big, golden eyes," Sabrina said. "They are warm and friendly. But there is also a touch of sadness in them. Her skin is like rose petals, soft and velvety."

"She's quite large," Demetra added. "Bigger than you, Hapgood. But that doesn't slow her down in the water."

Emily nodded. "She moves very fast and

very gracefully through Blue Lake. We think she's beautiful."

Sabrina was glad to see her cousins had changed their minds about the Blue Lake Monster. Now that they knew Oona, they admired and loved her, too.

Sabrina squinted out over the lake. "It's too bad we don't have any food. I was hoping Oona would join us for lunch."

"If it's food you need," Roxanne said, "I've got just the thing. Happy, show my cousins what we've brought."

Hapgood unfolded one large red wing. Underneath were two huge picnic baskets.

"Happy packed us a wonderful lunch," Roxanne explained. "There's food enough for everyone."

Sabrina clapped her hands together. "This is wonderful news! Zazz!" she called to the butterfly. "Hurry and tell everyone that our picnic celebration is about to begin. I have something I have to do."

Zazz flew to the gilliwags, who were napping in the reeds. Then she zoomed to the nymphs, who were frolicking in the pool at the base of Bluebonnet Falls. Then she flew to find the striders. They were skating near the shore of Blue Lake.

Gurt the gilliwag spread a tablecloth on the grass and set out the royal china. Demetra, Emily, and Roxanne unpacked the picnic baskets.

While everyone prepared for their feast, Sabrina looked for Oona.

She found her in the murky waters near the Willow-That-Weeps. Oona clutched the golden basket in her mouth.

"What are you doing?" Sabrina gasped. "Don't you remember? That basket is poisoned!"

Oona set the basket on a floating log. "I'm going to take this basket with its poisoned food to the bottom of our lake."

Sabrina's eyes widened. "Below the Deep Dark?"

Oona nodded. "I'm taking it to a place so deep that no creature will ever find it."

"But won't you join our picnic first?" Sabrina asked. "Roxanne brought an entire feast."

Oona smiled. "I would love to join your

feast. But first, I want to make sure that Lord Bleak doesn't harm one more creature in our beautiful lake. Then I'll return."

Sabrina stepped onto the floating log near the lake creature. She wrapped her arms around Oona's neck. "You've done much to help us. Is there any way we can repay your kindness?"

Oona closed her eyes in thought. When she opened them again she said, "I have been so lonely for so long. The best gift you could give me is your friendship."

"Of course!" Sabrina promised. "You will always have my friendship."

With that, Oona scooped up the poisoned basket and plunged into the lake.

Sabrina stared at the ripple of water where Oona had just been.

And for one moment, Sabrina was certain she saw a mermaid with sea-green eyes and skin the color of pearls.

Read the next sparkling adventure in

the Jewel Kingdom series!

JEWEL KINGDOM

The Emerald Princess
Plays a Trick

Turn the page for a special sneak peek!

1

EMILY THE COURT JESTER

Princess Emily slowly peeked around the trunk of the big elm tree. From where she hid, she could see Staghorn, the palace gardener. He was trimming the mulberry bushes that lined the path to her home in the Greenwood.

"Watch this," Emily whispered to her friend Arden, who stood a few feet behind her. "This is going to be *so* funny!"

Staghorn aimed his clippers at a small bush. Just as he snapped them shut, Emily tugged on the string she was holding. The bush leaped away from the dwarf.

"Hey!" Staghorn cried, nearly falling backward. "What's going on?"

Emily covered her mouth. Her green eyes sparkled. Her red hair shook with laughter.

Staghorn adjusted the glasses perched on the end of his nose. "My eyes must be playing tricks on me," he muttered.

He opened his clippers again, leaned toward the bush, and snapped the blades together.

Emily tugged on the string once more. The bush sprang in the air.

"Whoa!" Staghorn fell forward.

Emily couldn't help it. She burst out laughing.

"Hey!" Staghorn shouted, rubbing his nose. "What's so funny?"

Emily danced out from behind the tree.

Staghorn's face turned a bright red. "Princess Emily!" he cried. "I didn't see you."

"Of course not, Staghorn," Emily said with a giggle. She gave him a big hug. "I was hiding."

His furry eyebrows met in a frown. "Then it was *you* who made the bush hop away from me?"

"Yes!" Emily showed him the string she'd attached to the bush. "Wasn't that funny?"

Staghorn stared up at the Emerald Princess for a long time. "Yes, Princess," he said finally. "It was very funny."

Emily pointed at him. "You should have

seen the look on your face when the bush leaped in the air."

"I'm sure I looked very surprised," Staghorn said, brushing off the knees of his brown trousers.

"You looked positively silly!" Emily declared.

"I'm glad I made you laugh." Staghorn gestured down the path. "Now if you'll excuse me, I had better get on with my work. I have to do some pruning in the Twisted Vines."

Emily hugged the little man once more. "Thank you, my dear Staghorn. You are a very good sport!"

She watched the dwarf hurry off into the trees. The she turned to Arden. "Wasn't that fun?"

The beautiful white unicorn blinked her brown eyes. "I think it may have been fun for you. But I'm not so sure about Mr. Staghorn."

"Oh, he loves tricks," Emily said, picking a tiny bluebell and braiding it into Arden's mane. "Staghorn is like a grandfather to me. I've been teasing him since I was a little girl at the Jewel Palace."

Emily and her three cousins grew up in the Jewel Palace. It sat at the heart of the Jewel Kingdom.

"Did you see his face?" Arden asked.

Emily shrugged. "Staghorn always looks a little grumpy. That's why he's so much fun to play tricks on."

A bell chimed high above them. It came

from the Emerald Palace, a magnificent tree house held up by six huge cedar trees.

On the tip of one of the pinecone-covered turrets was a carved wooden clock. Emily had been given the clock by the people of the Greenwood when she was crowned the Emerald Princess.

Ding-ding-ding!

The clock chimed again.

"Did you hear that, Arden?" Emily asked. "It must be noon."

Arden turned her head. "Weren't you supposed to meet Princess Roxanne now?"

Emily's big green eyes widened. She covered her mouth with her hand. "I almost forgot! We're supposed to meet at the edge of the Greenwood."

Princess Roxanne was the Ruby Princess, and she lived high in the Red Mountains. Roxanne had been visiting Demetra, the Diamond Princess. Demetra was the oldest cousin. She ruled the White Winterland.

"Arden, would you mind giving me a ride?" Emily asked. "We'll reach the border much quicker that way."

"Hop on, Princess." Arden ducked her head and bent one knee.

Emily hiked up her green velvet skirt and hopped onto the unicorn's back.

"I have a special surprise for my cousin." Princess Emily patted the small package she held in her lap. "But I need to be at the border before Princess Roxanne."

"Surprise?" Arden asked as she cantered

beneath the rustling leaves of the Green-wood. "What is it?"

Emily bent close to the unicorn's ear and whispered, "If I told you, it wouldn't be a surprise." She patted her friend's neck. "Now let's hurry, please!"

Arden broke into a gallop. She leaped lightly over a fallen log, then ducked under a low-hanging branch.

Emily threw her head back and flung her arms out to the sides. "What a wonderful day!"

ABOUT THE AUTHORS

JAHNNA N. MALCOLM stands for Jahnna "and" Malcolm. Jahnna Beecham and Malcolm Hillgartner are married and write together. They have written over a hundred books for kids. Jahnna and Malcolm have written books and musicals about ballerinas, horses, ghosts, singing cowgirls, and magic.

Before Jahnna and Malcolm wrote books, they were actors. They met on the stage where Malcolm was playing a prince. And they were married on the stage where Jahnna was playing a princess.

Now they have their own prince and princess: Dash and Skye, who are almost grown up. They live in Oregon with their golden retriever, Archie.

If you want to learn more about them and hear songs from their musicals, including "The Best Christmas Pageant Ever: The Musical," visit jahnnanmalcolm.com.

Who says princesses have to be perfect?

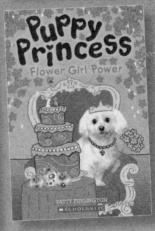

Join Princess Rosie and Cleo the kitten as they go on fun adventures around Petrovia!

Oh my glaciers, Diary!

Princess Lina is the *coolest* girl in school!